Who Did This?

By K. T. Hao • Illustrated by Poly Bernatene

Purple Bear Books • New York

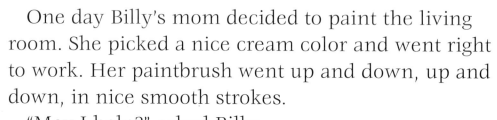

One day Billy's mom decided to paint the living room. She picked a nice cream color and went right to work. Her paintbrush went up and down, up and down, in nice smooth strokes.

"May I help?" asked Billy.

"No, sweetheart," she said. "Why don't you and Booboo play on the sofa and stay away from the paint."

Painting was hard work. After a few hours Mom took a break. She stretched out on the sofa and, before she knew it, she was fast asleep.

"Let's surprise Mom and finish painting," Billy said to Booboo.

At first, Billy painted just like his mom, up and down, up and down, in nice smooth strokes.

"This is boring," said Billy, so he started to paint a picture on the wall. He painted a house, a sun, some grass, and a boy standing in the front yard.

Billy stepped back to admire his picture and hit the ladder.

BUMP!

The ladder knocked down his mom's pretty china!

CRASH!

The ladder kept falling and smashed a lamp and a
vase . . .

BANG!

and landed on the sofa.

THUMP!

Billy's mom leaped up. She couldn't believe her eyes.

"Who did this?" she asked angrily.
"Er . . . ah . . . Booboo did it," said Billy.

Then she saw the picture painted on the wall.
"And *who* did *this*?" she demanded.

"Booboo did it," said Billy.

Mom was furious, but before she could start yelling,
their neighbor Mr. Pickles walked in.

"Who wants Mr. Pickles's famous cake?" he asked,
looking around. "Oh, seems like you've been busy."

Then Mr. Pickles noticed the picture on the wall. "Wow!" he said. "Who did this?"

"Booboo did it," said Billy.

"What a talented dog!" said Mr. Pickles, patting Booboo on the head. "I can't wait to tell everyone about such an amazing artist."

And tell everyone he did! Soon reporters arrived to see Booboo, the Amazing Artist.

They wrote newspaper and magazine articles about him, and Booboo was invited to perform on a popular television show.

The television studio was packed with fans, eager to see Booboo, the Amazing Artist. They surrounded Booboo, snapping his picture and shaking his paw.

Booboo was led onto the stage where an easel had been set up.

The crowd applauded. "Draw, draw, draw!" they cheered.

But Booboo just sat there, confused and scared, because, of course, he didn't really know how to draw. Soon the crowd's cheers turned to boos, which made Booboo so nervous he peed on the floor.

Booboo was devastated!

He headed home with his tail between his legs and flopped on the porch.

Billy felt terrible about poor Booboo. He fixed him a special dinner to cheer him up, but Booboo was too depressed to eat.

Later that evening, Booboo suddenly perked up. He sniffed the air and jumped to his feet. What was that smell?

Booboo raced off the porch, following the smell straight to Mr. Pickles's house. He leaped through the kitchen window, scattering dishes everywhere.

Booboo ran into the living room and saw that the curtains were on fire!

He wasted no time, jumping onto the sofa and peeing out the fire.

Billy and his mom also smelled the smoke and rushed over to Mr. Pickles's house.

"Are you all right?" asked Billy's mom.

"Oh, yes, indeed, thanks to Booboo."

Booboo

"Booboo, my hero!" exclaimed Mr. Pickles. "I can't wait to tell everyone how you saved my life!"

News traveled fast. The reporters returned to see Booboo, the Amazing Firefighter. His story appeared in newspapers and magazines, on radio and television. And this time, Booboo really *did* do it!

First published in Taiwan by Grimm Press

First English-language edition published in 2008 by Purple Bear Books Inc., New York

For more information about our books, visit our website: purplebearbooks.com

Library of Congress Cataloging-in-Publication Data is available.

This edition prepared by Cheshire Studio.

Printed in Taiwan

Trade edition

ISBN-10: 1-933327-32-4

ISBN-13: 978-1-933327-32-7

1 3 5 7 9 TE 10 8 6 4 2

Library edition

ISBN-10: 1-933327-33-2

ISBN-13: 978-1-933327-33-4

1 3 5 7 9 LE 10 8 6 4 2